from The Very Hungry Caterpillar

Eric Carle

PUFFIN

Christmas

is a time . . .

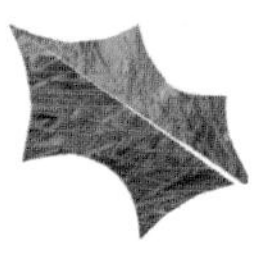

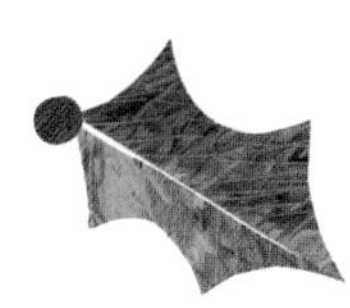

of

sparkle

and

shine.

We give gifts

with love...

and receive
them with joy.

We share

with others . . .

and

feast

till we're

full!

At the first sight
of snow...

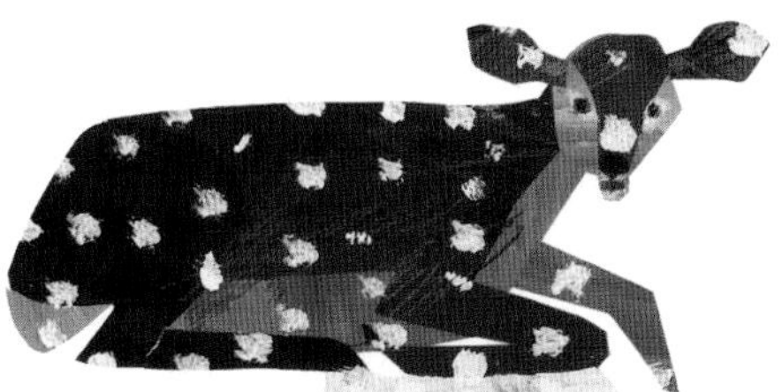

we rush out

to play.

And as the

night

falls . . .

we wait in peace...

for the most

magical

moment!

HA
CHRIS

PPY
TMAS

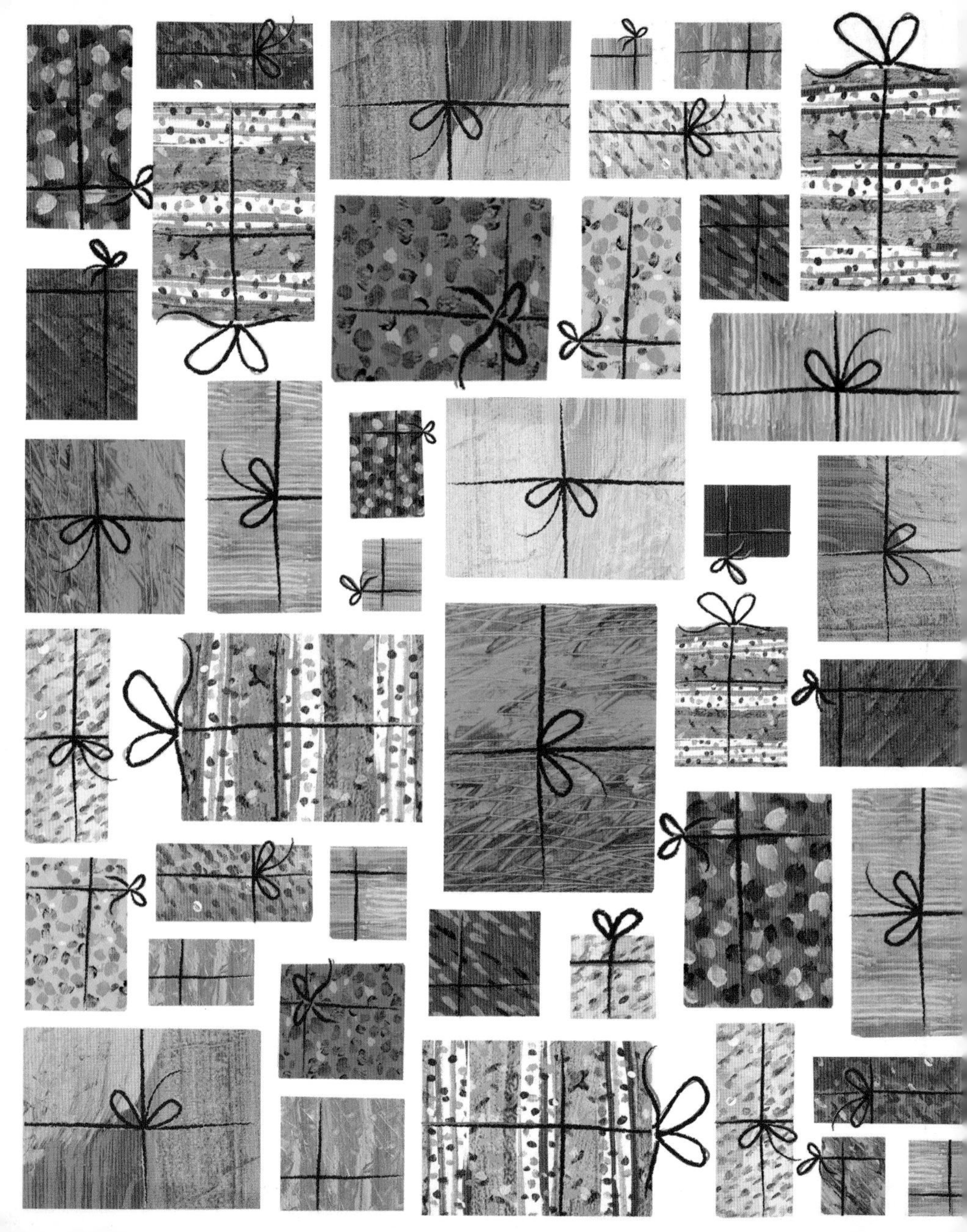